Kazuo Iwamura

# HOORAY for SNOW!

NorthSouth
New York / London

Early one morning, Mick, Mack, and Molly pushed open the window and peered outside. Their eyes grew big and round. During the night, something soft and white had covered everything in the forest. SNOW!

They scampered outside, making little round footprints everywhere they went.

"Let's get the sled!" shouted Mick.

Papa poked his head out the door. "B-r-r-r-r," he said. "It's *cold* out here! Come in and get some warm clothes."

"And some breakfast," said Mama.

Mick, Mack, and Molly ate as fast as they could.
Then they pulled on their sweaters and their socks
and their warm woolen caps.

"Come play in the snow with us, Papa," said Mick.

"B-r-r-r-r," said Papa. "Too cold for me."

"Come play in the snow with us, Mama," said Mack.

"I have too much work to do," said Mama.

"Push harder!" shouted Mick.

"Pull harder!" Molly shouted back.

"We're hardly moving," said Mack. "We need Papa."

"Come on, Papa!" said Mick. "Give us a pull."
"Then you can have a turn," said Molly.

"Hurry up, Papa!" said Mack.
"B-r-r-r-r-r," said Papa.

Mick, Mack, and Molly jumped onto the sled. Papa
ran through the snow, pulling the sled behind him.
"Faster, Papa! Faster!" shouted Mack.

"You want to go faster, eh?" said Papa. "Okay. Hang on!"
And he pushed the sled down the hill.
"Whoopeee!" shouted Mick and Molly.
"Help!" shouted Mack.

The three squirrels tumbled into the snow.

Papa came running. When he saw they were
all right, be began to laugh.

"You look like three snowmen!" he said.
"Here, Mack. You can wear my scarf. It's good
for a snowboy but it's too warm for me."

"I'm warming up," said Papa when they had
climbed back to the top of the hill. He gave
Molly his hat, then hopped onto the sled.
"Now it's my turn!"

*Whooooosh!* Papa flew down the hill.

*Whaaammm!* Papa sailed into a snowdrift.

Mick, Mack, and Molly raced down the
hill laughing.

"Now Papa's a snowman!" they shouted.

"I'll pull you back up," said Papa. "But take my coat,
Mick. I'm really hot."

"No wonder!" said Mick, Mack, and Molly.

"I have an idea!" said Papa suddenly. "I'll be right back."

Soon he returned with Mama.

"I don't have time for this," she said. "B-r-r-r-r.
You must be freezing!"

"We're not cold at all!" said Mick, Mack, and Molly.
"Hurry up, Mama."

"You'll warm right up," said Papa. "Sledding is a
warm business."

"Hooray for Mama!" shouted Mick.

"Hooray for Papa!" shouted Mack.

Then all together they shouted, "HOORAY FOR SNOW!"

First published in Japan in 1983 by Shiko-Sha Co., Ltd., Tokyo,
under the title *Yukinohiwa Atsui Atsui*.
Published in the United States, Great Britain, Canada, Australia, and New Zealand in 2008
by North-South Books Inc., an imprint of NordSüd Verlag AG, CH-8005 Zürich, Switzerland.
Distributed in the United States by North-South Books Inc., New York 10001.

Library of Congress Cataloging-in-Publication Data is available.
ISBN: 978-0-7358-2219-1 (trade edition).
10  9  8  7  6  5  4  3  2
Printed in China

www.northsouth.com